Blick auf die Allgäuer Alpen

WALK ON MOON

ASTRONAUTS LAND ON PLAIN;
COLLECT ROCKS, PLANT FLAG

Marconi

THE FRANK SHOW

David Mackintosh

ABRAMS BOOKS FOR YOUNG READERS

New York

...aloging-in-Publication Data has been applied for and
...y be obtained from the Library of Congress.
...N: 978-1-4197-0393-5

...t and illustrations copyright © 2012 David Mackintosh
...k designed and lettered by David Mackintosh

...st published in hardcover in Great Britain by
...rperCollins Children's Books in 2012.
...rperCollins Children's Books is a division of
...rperCollins Publishers Ltd.

Printed and bound by Printing Express, Hong Kong
10 9 8 7 6 5 4 3 2 1

For bulk discount inquiries, contact
specialsales@abramsbooks.com.

THE ART OF BOOKS SINCE 1949

115 West 18th Street
New York, NY 10011
www.abramsbooks.com

My grandpa's name is Frank.

Frank lives at our house, and he's always around.

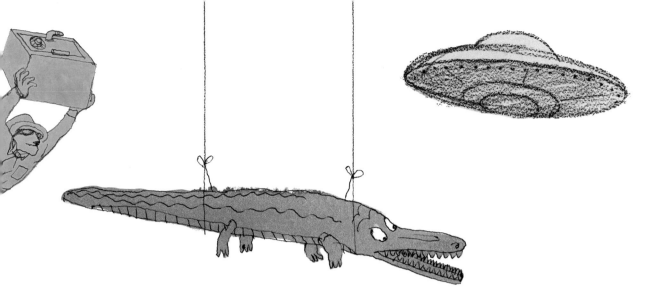

Frank talks about what things were like when he was a boy my age. He says, "Things were a lot tougher back then."

Frank says that it was a lot quieter when he was my age.
"*You could hear yourself think!*" he yells.

My teacher has asked us to talk about a member of our family for show-and-tell on Friday. We can choose one person and talk for one minute, about the things they like and what kind of person they are.

I ask Mom if I can talk about her, but she says that she is very busy and that I should speak to my father when he gets off the phone.

Dad says why don't I talk about Minnie, my sister? Minnie won't make a good subject to talk about, so I tell him I'll think about it.

The only person left is Frank.
But Frank is just a grandpa.

Frank always says,

"These days there are too many gadgets and gizmos. I prefer doing things the old-fashioned way."

Prehistoric

Today I told my teacher that Mom was very busy and Dad had had a very long day, so the only person left in my family to talk about was Frank, my grandpa.
She said, "*Fabulous!*" But I don't know about that.

At home, Frank says he doesn't like "fancy" food.
"Plain and simple, that's me," he reckons.

I wonder if there is *anything* about Frank that will make my talk interesting.

On Tuesday at the barbershop, Frank says he only needs to get his hair cut once a year and he doesn't trust barbers. He says, "If it ain't broke, don't fix it. I can do without their input."

And I just have mine tidied up.

My friend Tom says that his uncle Marlon is a musician who plays drums on the radio. Tom says he's allowed to bring his drumsticks on Friday. *His uncle is cool.*

That night, I ask Frank if he can play a musical instrument. Maybe the electric guitar?

Frank says, "Today's music is just noise, and you can't understand the words."

He only likes
listening to
his music
and says,

"**They
don't
make
'em
like
that
anymore.**"

Barbara Bailey told me that she's going to bring a
photo of her grandma's deluxe mobility scooter.
She's a retiree and secretary of a bridge club.

Maybe I should take
a photo of Frank?

That night, I ask Frank why
he doesn't drive a scooter
or play bridge.

Frank says, "Doctors speak a lot of mumbo jumbo,
and bridge is dull as old dishwater."

He doesn't trust doctors as far as he can throw them,
which isn't far on account of his arm.
And one of his hips.

Kristian's dad is a comedian on TV who makes everyone laugh. Paolo's mom is Italian and knows all about Italian and can speak Italian. Fay's cousin tells you if your bag's too heavy at the airport. Donny's dad works in a potato chip factory. Saul's aunt swam the English Channel. Hugo's stepbrother has a sports car, with an eight-ball gearshift knob.

My grandpa's arm
hurts when it's
about to rain.

I wish I could choose Tom. He's my age and I've known him since January. Tom carries a full deck of Modern Marvels flash cards in his back pocket, and I'm the only other person he lets hold them. He's smaller than me, but that doesn't matter when you're best friends.

Tom asked me why I chose Frank for my talk,
because Frank's just a grandpa.

I didn't know what to say.

So now Tom and me aren't speaking.

On the way home, I don't care if Tom thinks Frank isn't a good show-and-tell. Tom doesn't know Frank like I do and doesn't even live at my house with my family. So what does he know?

388 OAP

But then, Tom might be right,
because everyone has someone
interesting to talk about. And Frank is,
well . . . just my grandpa.

My grandpa doesn't always like the way things are.
And he always does things his way.

He doesn't like noise, **or** today's music, **or** gadgets and gizmos (**or** new things), **or** haircuts, **or** weather, **or** doctors, **or** any sort of ice cream that isn't vanilla. **And** today I have to talk all about him for a *full minute*.

In class, everyone is excited.

They have all spoken for a full minute each about a member of their family, even Clive Martin. Then we all have to look out of the window to see Hannah's mom's company car.

Everyone in my class has someone
interesting to show and tell.

But now it's my turn to talk about . . .

Frank.

I tell them everything I know about Frank . . .

how Frank doesn't like noise, **or** today's music,
or gadgets and gizmos (**or** new things), **or** haircuts,
or weather, **or** doctors, **or** anything but vanilla,
and about how everything was a lot tougher when
he was a boy my age.

And . . . *that's it.*

I've run out of things I can say about Frank,
and everyone is looking straight at me,

when . . .

Frank begins to tell a story about how he led an
army in a charge across a muddy battlefield . . .

with bullets
whistling all around
like African bees . . .

and how the whole
way he didn't miss
a single note on
his bugle . . .

except when an
explosion made
him play a sharp
instead of a flat . . .

and how he
gave his last
drop of water to
a thirsty horse . . .

and captured one hundred enemy soldiers with
nothing but his wit and brute force . . .

and how later . . . he and his buddies had a green
tattoo put on their arms to remember that day.

Frank explains how he has a piece of metal
left in his elbow from when he was in the war.
"And every time it's about to rain,
I know because my arm goes numb."

Sheldon Robe asks if getting a
blurry tattoo hurts, and
Frank winks and says,
"You bet it did, *hombre.*"

Then we all have lunch.

*He is older,
than all of
our birthdays
added up.*

And everybody cheered for my grandpa Frank and me.

On the way home, Tom asked if he could visit Frank and me at our house one day and I said, "You bet you can, *hombre*."